THE MAKING OF A LEADER

AN INSPIRING TALE FOR YOUNG WOMEN

A proud sponsor of the
Green Supercamp™ Australia Program
http://www.greensupercamp.com.au/

OTHER PRODUCTS BY JULIE LEWIN

BOOKS

Author

AreekeerA® Vibration: Healing Yourself From Within
AreekeerA® Celestial Guidance Oracle Deck

Co-Author

Procrastination Begone: 11 Ways to SPARK Your Motivation &
Light Up Your Business

Luminicious: 10 Inspirational Stories and Practices to Ignite Your
Feminine Power and Own Your Light!

Life Sucks But You Can Turn It Around

Your Well-Being Sorted!

AUDIO

Before After Surgery Toolbox
Conquer Anxiety Program

MEDITATIONS

Sacred Garden
Chakra Magic
Dolphin Swim
Energy Sensitivity
Regeneration Sleep
Kids Sleep

www.julielewin.com

THE MAKING OF A LEADER

AN INSPIRING TALE FOR YOUNG WOMEN

JULIE LEWIN

Medical Intuitive, Leader of Women

Celestial
Consciousness
PUBLISHING

Cover Design by Tash Lewin / Stephanie Kakris

Book Design by Tash Lewin

Cover photography by Allef Vinicius on Unsplash

National Library of Australia

Cataloguing-in-Publication entry:

Lewin, Julie, 1959-

The Making of a Leader / Julie Lewin

1st ed.

ISBN: 978-0-9874957-3-0

1. Leader. 2. Community. 3. Death. 4. Bullying

Published by Celestial Consciousness Publishing
PO Box 1142, Milton BC Qld 4064
Email: support@julielewin.com
Phone: +61 421 542 436

To wonderful husband Frank, for your enormous support.

A special thank you to my mother and late grandmother for all their patience and wisdom throughout my life. My grandmother wrote the poem at the back of the book.

Thank you Tarryn, Lynne, Sandy and Tash for editing my drafts and giving me honest, constructive feedback. You provoked me to continually dig deeper to create Maggie into a real character.

Tash your support as my graphic designer and book designer is so appreciated. You inspire me to give my best - always.

INTRODUCTION

This story is framed around my incredible journey and some of the lessons experienced along the way.

Although Maggie is a created character, she is a mixture of my experiences, my observations of life and pure fiction.

My hope is that Maggie will inspire you to make a difference with your life, if you are not already living to your full potential.

This simple story has been written in a style which

at times seems exaggerated and perhaps unbelievable. This is deliberate. My intention is to magnify situations and move you to consider your life, how you think, and what actions you take unconsciously every day to create your world.

This story is about the primary emotions – fear, sorrow and anger. The experience of LOVE is not a constant in the lives of most human beings, but LOVE is the emotion everyone seeks. Underlying the fleeting experiences of love and happiness are the three primary emotions that people try to avoid ie., fear, sorrow and anger.

Emotion is simply energy and when this is truly understood any emotion can be conducted (ie., used in a constructive, focused way) to create positive change. Think about a time you have been so angry you had to do something or you would explode. You either chose to do something violent, or you channelled that energy into doing something constructive.

When you find yourself in a situation you don't like, ask yourself the question – "Am I conducting my energy in the best possible way?" Be totally honest with yourself and make positive life choices based on your answer. By doing this, you open yourself up to a new level of existence.

My hope is that as you read "The Making of a Leader" you experience a journey through each of the primary emotions and are awakened to a world different to the one you presumed you lived in.

Julie Lewin

Medical Intuitive | Leader of Women

CHAPTER 1

Maggie had always felt like an outsider. She believed she didn't fit in anywhere. She felt tolerated, but not welcome. She seemed to drift through her childhood, yet not really participate in the drama going on around her. To protect herself, she was forever escaping into her own world and further alienating herself from her classmates.

The most painful realisation for Maggie was the shattering of her illusion that if people were nice to her, they were good people and her friends. She was ashamed that her naivety and trusting nature put her into situations of gross bullying.

Today was no exception. Maggie stood at the edge of the cool group hoping they would include her in the conversation.

Shanna stopped speaking, raised one eyebrow and stared disdainfully at her. No words were necessary to tell Maggie she shouldn't be there. As she turned and started to walk away, Shanna shuddered and whispered in a loud voice so Maggie would hear, "She is so eeuugghhh and her clothes! What century is she from anyway? I can't stand the way she hangs around us all the time – like a bird waiting for a crumb!"

The girls snickered, not game to say anything else because they didn't want to be excluded from the group. This hurt more than Shanna's comments. Maggie missed the sympathetic looks on some of the girls' faces because she had already turned away.

--

Looking at her reflection in the bathroom mirror, Maggie silently screamed at herself, "Uuugggghhhh, you are so fat and ugly – you have no personality – you have nothing to say – it's no wonder you have no friends and no one likes you AT ALL!!! Who do you think you are anyway? How dare you even try to be part of that group! They don't like you and they NEVER will. You are not worth it!!!!"

Maggie stared at herself in the mirror – looking for something, anything that would ease her pain.

Lost in her misery she slowly slid down the bathroom wall, curling up into a ball on the floor, rocking backwards and forwards, sobbing without making a sound. Eventually, she took a ragged breath and spoke out loud into the silent room.

"Oh God, why am I here? Why do I have to do this? This can't be all there is!"

--

Maggie started writing a diary in high school. It helped her feel less alone or left out. She found it was the one place she could be truly honest and knew no one else would find out what she thought or how she felt. It became her sanctuary and also her hell. She left nothing out. The first page of her new diary started with these words:

1.3.2000 – I'm 15 years old and I'm a freak! I feel so different from everyone else!

The other girls have pictures of their favourite singers and idols plastered all over their walls like a mural. (Dad would never let me do that!) Some of them have "KEEP OUT" signs on their doors. (And that would be asking for trouble!) They spend a lot of money on magazines and clothes, and all they want to talk about is boys! (Why???)

There must be something wrong with me – I'm not like that! Does that mean I'm a lesbian??? Dear God, I don't know! All I know is I definitely don't belong here!

I don't understand half of what Mum says, so she doesn't really help me. But thankfully Grandma always seems to know what to say, even when I don't know what I need the answer to.

I wrote to Grandma today hoping she would help me.

"Dear Grandma,

I'm so unhappy. Why don't the girls at school like me? I don't know what I do to annoy them. I know I'm different to them, but they could let me be part of the group – couldn't they? I want to be liked – and they don't want me anywhere near them.

I know I don't dress like them, and I guess the way I wear my hair isn't very attractive, but it's easy to look after. Even though I can't think of anything to say when I'm near them doesn't mean they have to be horrible to me, does it?

I feel stupid and ugly and a nobody.

I don't feel like I'm a girl – because I'm not interested in the things they're always talking about – boys, music or clothes – but I want to feel like a girl!

They know the words to all the latest songs and all about the people who sing them. I can't even understand the words to the songs, let alone remember them. They all go to the movies and know all about the actors. I forget what happened in a movie as soon as I walk out of the theatre, so I don't even bother going.

Do you think if I pretended to be interested in those things they would let me be part of the group?

Grandma even though I'm not like them, I still want to fit in.

Another thing – they are always saying horrible things about their mothers. I can't understand this! I know Mum can be a pain, but I don't say horrible things about her to other people.

Please write soon. I need your help.

All my love, Maggie"

8.3.2000 – It's now 7 days and no letter from Grandma. Did I say something I shouldn't have? Am I really such a bad person? I can't understand why she hasn't written!

Maggie locked her diary and hid it at the back of her wardrobe, behind her clothes. Feeling sad she went downstairs to the kitchen and helped her mother prepare the vegetables for dinner.

"Mum, I wrote to Grandma over a week ago and she hasn't written back yet! She's never taken this long to answer my letters before."

"Honey, I don't know why she hasn't written. You know Grandma – she lives by her own rules. Maybe she's busy. I'm sure she'll write when she has a spare minute. Did you write her about anything important?”

“Yes.”

“Anything you want to share with me?”

“No!”

“Oh! Okay. Honey, just because you decide you want something right now doesn’t mean it’s the right time for you. Maybe the letter Grandma’s going to write to you will come at a time when you really need it. Patience Maggie – your letter will come.”

“But she always writes back straight away!” Maggie emphasises “straight away” by stamping her right foot. Her mother, Rose, ignored her, and calmly continued the conversation as if nothing had happened which really annoyed Maggie.

"Yes honey, she usually does, but this time she hasn't. Maybe she has to think about how to answer your questions. Have you thought about that?"

Maggie snapped back at her mother, "Of course not! I haven't had to before."

Rose looked at Maggie and raised her eyebrows. She was shocked at her behaviour and thought something is really out of balance here.

"Maggie are you sure there isn't something you want to talk to me about?"

"No MUM! I want to hear what Grandma has to say!"

"Maggie, I don't need to listen to you speaking this way, go and have a think about what you're doing right now."

Looking startled by her mother's tone and what she said, a sudden dawning of understanding spread across Maggie's face, "Oh my God Mum, I've only been thinking of myself and what I want, haven't I?"

"Hmm, yes Maggie, you have. I hope you've learned something here. This is a moment to remember. What you have just discovered is the very thing everyone tends to do unconsciously."

"What do you mean?"

"Think only about themselves! Most people look at a situation through one lens – the lens that is about them. This becomes the blueprint for their memory which is then anchored into their mind by the emotion they are feeling at that time."

Maggie groans, "Muuuummmm, I know you are trying to help me, but you just confuse me. I'm going to wait for Grandma's letter and see what she says. I don't want to listen to you talk about that stuff right now. It's too weird!"

There was silence for a minute and Maggie apologetically said, "Umm, actually that wasn't a very nice thing to say, was it? I'm sorry Mum. You're not angry with me because I want to wait for Grandma's letter are you?"

Rose sighed, wondering what she could say to Maggie that would help her.

"Sweetheart no, I'm not angry with you, but I want you to listen to me very carefully. You need to know that I love you and will always love you no matter what you do or say or what happens to you.

I want you to also understand I respect who you are and the choices you make. I trust and believe you are a young woman who understands she can make any choices she wants to, but who also knows she must accept responsibility for her choices.

When you make a choice with insight you are living your destiny. When you make a choice without thinking about the consequences of that choice, sometimes you will be safe, yet you run the risk of danger, heartache, loss of some kind, or some other outcome that could last minutes, hours, days or a lifetime and makes you question or regret that choice.

I have faith in you and I have faith in the Divine Mystery that guides all our lives. Maggie, I know you haven't had an easy time growing up, particularly in high school, and I'm really sorry I can't take your pain away for you, but that's not my job!

You need to dig inside yourself and grow stronger through your difficult times. If you can, look at situations from another perspective. And, please, always know I'm very proud of you."

Feeling bad because she'd been grumpy, Maggie managed to say sheepishly, "I feel really bad about what I said. Thanks for not being angry with me. You've shown me I don't have to let words hurt me."

She gave her mother a big hug and said, "I'm sorry I've been awful today. I'm really glad you're my Mum."

Maggie went to her room to think about what her mother had said and to write in her diary again.

8.3.2000 (cont) – How bad am I !!!!! I've never thought of that before – that Grandma could have other things she needed to do before she wrote to me. Or, even that she would need to think about what she wrote to me. I thought she knew everything and whenever I wanted something from her – she would give it to me straight away!

I feel very selfish now. I can see life is not all about me and what I want.

What was it Mum said about faith? Could that really be what I'm being asked to do now? Have faith that Grandma will answer my letter in the right time.

The www.dictionary.com website says that "faith" is:

Confident belief in the truth, value, or trustworthiness of a person, idea, or thing.

Belief that does not rest on logical proof or material evidence.

Loyalty to a person or thing; allegiance, keeping faith with one's supporters.

Often Faith Christianity. The theological virtue defined as secure belief in God and a trusting acceptance of God's will.

The body of dogma of a religion: the Muslim faith.

A set of principles or beliefs.

Huh ... I never knew it was all of those things.

I really need to think about everything Mum's just told me – man, I can't believe I've been so selfish.

Oh yeah, that's right – poor me – nobody loves me.

Well, I've just been told that's not true, so what else do I believe that's not true?

10.3.2000 – Get over yourself Maggie! Whatever it takes!!!! Never again do I want to feel like I did the day I wrote to Grandma. So if I stop thinking about myself and what I want all the time – focus on what I can do for others or even the Earth some of the time – then maybe I won't worry about feeling different from the other girls.

That's it!!! I'll take a vow, right here and now.

Maggie loved to lie in the backyard on a blanket in the middle of the night. When she was in the garden with the stars, she didn't feel so lonely. It was her sanctuary away from pain and rejection.

After writing her vow in her diary, Maggie stood up

tall, raised her face to the stars and in a hushed voice solemnly declared:

"Dear Universe, starting right now – I promise to focus my energy on serving others and the World every day in some way, shape or form that allows my heart to connect with my life purpose. I have faith I will be guided in the best use of my time from this moment forward so I may always serve in your Light."

Maggie's journey of discovery into how she could help her community began. She started by going to her local library. It had all sorts of information about the community.

The library didn't give her the answer she was looking for though, so she made a list of all the things she liked to do or would like to do. She was amazed at what she actually wrote down. By doing this she discovered a way of always remembering the lesson

about being selfish.

CHAPTER 2

15.3.2000 – I still can't believe it!!!! I don't care what the other girls think! I don't care that Grandma hasn't written! An amazing thing happened today. I won't ever be the same again – I discovered something greater than me!!!

I remembered that Grandma enjoys me massaging hand cream into her hands and arms. Since Grandpa died she told me that she doesn't get touched very much by others in a way that feels nice. She lives in another State and I don't get to see her much to do this.

This got me thinking that there must be other grandmothers who don't see their grandchildren very often either.

Light bulb moment

Aha! That's it – maybe they would like me to visit and rub hand cream into their hands and arms.

But how frightening? Could I do this – really?

Well, Mum said she had faith in me. This helped me to feel the fear and push through it.

Once I did that everything fell into place as to what I needed to do next. I didn't tell anyone what I was going to do, because I was afraid they would think it was a stupid idea and say things like "it would never work" or "nobody will let you do that!". I think Mum calls that "dream stealing".

There was more to it though than not wanting my dream stolen before it even began. I felt deep inside I wanted to have an idea and make it happen without help. This was very important to me.

I began to understand what Mum had been talking about – particularly when she'd say "truly connecting with your dream is a sacred journey".

I even had the courage to think about what the other girls at school were always talking about, so I went and bought some new clothes. Something modern! And I had my hair cut in a way that opened my face up and emphasised my eyes.

On March 15 2000, Maggie went to the nursing home in Dunedin Street with a new, soft, pink fluffy hand towel and a jar of rose scented hand cream (her Grandmother's favourite) tucked in her new white basket.

Although she was feeling nervous, she acted like she wasn't. She walked up to the reception desk with a big smile and said in a confident voice to the lady behind the desk, "Hello, my name is Maggie and I live close by in Terrence Road. Last week I discovered I've been thinking only about myself, and to help me remember this lesson, I've decided to do something for my community.

Of all the things I could do, I've decided I'd like to spend some time with the grandmothers who live here and don't see their grandchildren very often.

My Grandma, who lives in another State, enjoys me massaging hand cream into her hands and arms while we have a chat. Do you think I could come here after school for an hour and do the same for the grandmothers who don't see their grandchildren?"

With her heart beating painfully in her chest and blood pounding in her ears Maggie nervously waited for an answer.

With a twinkle in her eye that could have been the beginning of a tear catching the afternoon sun, Mrs Parkinson said, "Well, young Maggie what a wonderful story. Firstly, let me introduce myself, I'm Mrs Parkinson. I don't see any reason why you couldn't do that. Let me check with Matron first. I won't be long."

Negative thoughts crowded her mind, but she determinedly pushed them away. After about 10 minutes, Mrs Parkinson waddled slowly back to the reception desk and said, "Maggie, Matron said yes you can come here and see if it is something that will work for all of us. We have quite a number of grandmothers here who don't see their children or their grandchildren at all. Matron is sure some of them would love to have you visit."

Maggie sheepishly raised her new basket and put it on the counter.

Mrs Parkinson smiled knowingly, "Aaahhh, I see you've brought your basket with you. Would you like to start today?"

Maggie shouted a jubilant "YES!" and pumped her arm in the air.

"Yyyeeesss – thank you Mrs Parkinson. How fantastic! I was terrified you would say no.

When Mum said she had faith in me to make the right choices and that the way would be shown if I followed my heart, I wasn't sure if she was right. Now I feel as if I could do anything. It was faith that kept me going ahead with my plan, despite my fears I could be told no and feel devastated and even more of a failure.

Even though I was so afraid, something told me to keep going with my plans and ask! How FANTASTIC!!!! This time the answer is YES.

As I was growing up, Mum said to me, 'If you don't ask, the answer will always be no.' She was right!"

Mrs Parkinson chuckled to herself and said, "Maggie, I think we are going to get along just fine."

Maggie was feeling a little anxious when Mrs Parkinson led her into a beautiful pale pink room not far from reception.

Speaking a little louder than normal, Mrs Parkinson said, "Mrs Roberts, I want to introduce you to Maggie. She wants to spend some of her time after school with grandmothers who don't see their grandchildren. Would you like Maggie to sit with you?"

Mrs Roberts' eyes lit up like a sunbeam sparkling on a dewdrop in the morning light. She struggled to sit up in her bed so she could see what was happening.

"Would I? Oh yes please. That would be wonderful dear."

Mrs Parkinson moved close to Mrs Roberts and said in a caring voice, "Would you like Maggie to rub hand cream into your hands and arms as she sits and talks to you?"

"Ooooohhhhh, yes dear thank you. I would really like that. My Ben used to do that before he passed. I would really enjoy that Maggie, if you're sure you would like to do that for an old lady like me?"

Mrs Roberts shakily put her hand out to Maggie in a gesture of welcome. Maggie quickly stepped forward and took the graceful, thin, wrinkled hand in her own two young plump hands, feeling privileged to be given this opportunity.

Although Mrs Roberts was very old and wrinkled, the twinkle in her eyes and the delight on her face helped Maggie forget about that. It felt a little strange touching someone she didn't know, but Maggie found Mrs Roberts' skin to be very soft – almost fragile.

As she slowly rubbed cream into Mrs Roberts' hands Maggie could hear her mother's voice saying,

"When you give to another do so with all your heart and embrace the act as a sacred activity."

Until that moment, she hadn't a clue what her mother was talking about. Strangely though, Maggie soon found she entered a sacred space as she gently massaged the cream into Mrs Roberts' hands and arms. It was a strong feeling of connection and Maggie wondered if this was what "being at one with God" felt like.

They didn't speak very much. They didn't need to.

Mrs Roberts closed her eyes. She appeared to be sleeping. The room felt peaceful and filled with an unusual light. Maggie gently eased the fluffy pink hand towel from under Mrs Roberts' arm. She didn't move. Maggie quietly put the towel and hand cream into her basket and walked towards the door. With one last glance around the room she slipped through the door and pulled it shut behind her.

Maggie thought, "What … an … amazing … hour! It felt like 10 minutes."

She made her way down the corridor to where Mrs Parkinson was working.

Running the last few metres to the reception desk, Maggie jubilantly said in a mock whisper, "Mrs Parkinson, thaaannnkkkkk yoooouuuu ssssoooo much! Could you please thank Matron for me, too!"

Before Mrs Parkinson could respond, Maggie continued quickly without even drawing a breath, "Mrs Roberts is the sweetest woman. She reminds me of my Grandma. I would love to come back again."

Mrs Parkinson smiled broadly as Maggie stopped suddenly and drew a deep breath.

"Maggie I have a confession to make. While you were with Mrs Roberts I checked in to see how you were going. You sounded bright and confident when you asked if you could sit with our ladies, but I wanted to make sure you were okay and that Mrs Roberts wasn't feeling uncomfortable with you being there with her.

I was so amazed at what I saw that I called Matron down to have a look, too. I didn't tell you before, but Mrs Roberts hasn't had a visitor for 3 years and lately she hasn't been eating her meals either. She's been very sad and we thought we'd be losing her any time soon. I couldn't tell you the last time she smiled or took an interest in anything or anyone.

When we saw her smiling and the gentle, loving way you were massaging cream into her hands and arms, we knew you were an angel from God. Matron told me to tell you that if you wanted to come again, it would be a wonderful gift to the nursing home to have you here.

Thank you Maggie from both of us for the gift of love you have brought to the nursing home today."

Before Mrs Parkinson had finished speaking, tears were running down Maggie's face. She had no idea something so simple could make such a difference to someone's life. And it didn't just affect Mrs Roberts, it made a difference to Mrs Parkinson and Matron, too.

Through tears and a wobbly chin, Maggie said, "We really saw a miracle here today, didn't we? Thank you for telling me that Mrs Parkinson. I now know if I follow my heart, I will make the right choices."

Maggie looked behind Mrs Parkinson to the large clock on the wall and said, "Oh, is that the time? I have to go now and I will definitely be back tomorrow afternoon after school. Thank you again. Bye."

CHAPTER 3

Maggie ran all the way home, bubbling over with a new feeling which was difficult to describe. She felt explosions of energy throughout her body and was in awe that one experience could change the way she thought about everything.

She opened the gate and was halfway up the path before remembering she hadn't checked the letterbox to see if her letter had arrived. She ran back and slowly lifted the lid to look inside – it was there! A beautiful pink envelope with tiny butterflies all around the edges.

She'd written at last!

Maggie was so glad it was after she had figured out what to do. She felt more grown up now than she did when she wrote to her grandmother.

Maggie couldn't wait to read her letter and write more in her diary. She made a glass of Milo, took one of her mother's newly baked biscuits and went to the back corner of the garden where her grandmother said the fairies lived. Maggie's father loved his mother-in-law's stories, too. He built a beautiful seat and put it in the fairies' garden for when she came to stay, and for Maggie, too – when she remembered!

Breathing deeply, enjoying the smell of the garden, Maggie opened her letter with trembling fingers. She had been waiting so long to receive it. How amazing the letter arrived the very day Maggie had the courage to follow her dream and make it a reality.

"Darling Maggie,

It is always wonderful to get your letters, but I was sad to read you have been so unhappy. You are growing up fast into a young woman. My sorrow is that I can't be there to watch you grow.

Your letter reminded me of when I was 15 going on 16. (I know how much of a difference it is to be 'nearly 16'). Of course, things were different in my day, but the emotions a 15 year old girl experiences are as old as time.

The truth is Maggie I'm sure everyone feels they are different and in some way they don't fit in at times, even if they are in the 'cool group'.

You may be feeling different right now, but this can be a good thing, too. From my observation over the years, being in the 'cool group' tends to develop followers – not leaders. What you need to decide my dear is whether you want to be a follower or a leader.

There is a place for both – but what do YOU want to be?

Do you want to follow a group of girls, do things that don't seem to have any purpose, talk about things that don't seem to make any sense, and get emotionally mixed up with boys instead of growing up first; or do you want to be a leader of girls, inspiring them to give a part of their time to others rather than solely to themselves?

Do you want to have stimulating conversations that develop depth of character and grow you into a young woman who instinctively knows she doesn't need another to feel complete?

Do you want to experience the freedom to be in relationships with young men and women which are about sharing of energy, rather than struggling with neediness and demanding and taking energy?

Darling girl, if you can understand what I'm trying to say, the 'cool group' will want to have what you have. Not the other way around. You'll see!

Froth and bubble is okay in small doses, depth and passion is what sustains a relationship – any relationship. Not just that between a boy and girl or a man and woman.

Listen to your heart Maggie. Be true to your passion and people will see something about you that is different. You will be beautiful. There'll be a brightness, an attractiveness that can't be manufactured with 'designer clothes', 'fad jewellery', and 'trendy haircuts'.

Being true to your passion creates an aura about you that can't be bought. It is inspiring. It is magical – like the fairies in the bottom of the garden.

My dear Maggie, don't be afraid to be different. Be unique. Be an individual. Be a leader of women.

You'll be surprised at what happens when you embrace who you really are!!!

I look forward with anticipation to hearing your latest news.

Loving you dearly, Grandma."

*15.3.2000 (cont) – How fantastic was that!
Grandma's letter arrived after I had already started
doing what she had written about.*

Be a leader of women. I like that!

*What do I want to be – a leader or a follower?
Before today that would have been a difficult question
to answer, as I've never thought of myself as being a
leader. But something powerful happened today when I
found the courage to go to the nursing home and ask if I
could spend some time with the grandmothers.*

*I feel like a new person who I don't know yet. It's
going to be wonderful to discover who I really am.*

*Grandma's letter has helped me a lot, especially the
part about being a follower or a leader. I hadn't thought
about that before, but I can see now that I was really*

asking her how to become a follower and hope that the 'cool group' would let me in.

"Maggie, honey, are you home?"

Maggie closed her diary, grabbed her things off the seat and ran through the garden into the kitchen shouting, "Mum! Grandma wrote at last and just like I said, she always knows what to say."

"Hello my lovely," said Rose, wrapping her in a huge hug. "That's wonderful news. Sounds like Grandma's letter has made your day."

Rose pulled away from Maggie so she could look into her eyes and said with meaning, "Have you had a good day?"

Maggie slipped out of Rose's arms and said, "It's

been the best day I've ever had!"

Rose watched in surprise and delight at the enthusiasm in Maggie's voice. She hadn't heard that for a long time. A wave of relief washed through her to see her daughter's happy, beaming face and hear her infectious laughter filling the room. Maggie danced around the kitchen, barely able to contain her happiness.

"You'll never guess what I've done! It's been the most amazing day. You know how you told me not to let anyone steal my dreams?"

"Yes."

"Well, after we talked last week and I realised I'd only been thinking about myself when I wanted Grandma to write straight away, I decided to do some community service. I always want to remember this lesson.

Mum, you telling me you had faith in me meant a lot. I wouldn't have believed it if I hadn't experienced what's happened this last week."

"That's great news, Maggie. Tell me what you've done."

"After going to the library to see what community projects were being advertised there and not finding anything that inspired me, I thought about what I like to do and wrote a list of everything that made me feel connected in some way that would help my community. I put the list under my pillow and went to sleep asking God (yes, I know you never thought I would ever do that, did you?) to help me decide what the best use of my time would be in serving my community.

When I woke up, I knew I needed to go through my list and write on one side of a clean page all the things I could do without help from anyone else and on the other side all the things where I would need other people's help.

That night I put the new list under my pillow and asked God to help me choose whether I wanted to do something on my own or with help.

I remembered you telling me when making a decision to look into my heart and really consider what felt right for me, and then make my decision based on what I felt.

When I woke up the second morning, I knew I didn't need to make another list. I knew I wanted to go to the nursing home and spend time with the grandmothers who don't see their grandchildren very often."

Rose's eyes filled with tears. She didn't say anything, just looked at Maggie encouraging her to continue with her story.

"You'll never guess, Mum! I went to the nursing in Dunedin Street this afternoon. I was really scared, but pretended I wasn't and asked the lady on reception whose name is Mrs Parkinson if I could sit with the grandmothers and rub their hands and arms with cream. She asked Matron who said yes and well, that's what I did this afternoon.

Mum, I sat with Mrs Roberts. She is a little deaf and seems so old. She must be in her nineties. We didn't talk much, but I rubbed cream on her hands and arms which she loved. She reminded me of Grandma, but older. And it was easy to be with her. It didn't take long for me to feel comfortable and not afraid of her."

"Honey, come here. I am so very proud of you."

Rose wrapped her arms around Maggie and rocked from side to side giving her a delicious hug that made her feel very loved. Tears rolled down Rose's face and splashed onto Maggie's head. She didn't mind.

"Do you want to know the best part, Mum? Until I went there today, Mrs Roberts hadn't had a visitor for 3 years. Mrs Parkinson said she's been so sad and not eating they thought she might die soon."

Rose continued to look at Maggie with tear filled eyes, saying nothing, but encouraging her to keep talking about her day. Maggie could see her mother wanted to say things to her and was pleased she just listened, letting her finish telling her amazing story.

"Matron said I can come back to the nursing home every afternoon for an hour and sit with the grandmothers. What do you think Mum? Is it okay?"

Through her tears and emotional smile, Rose said in a tender voice, "Gorgeous girl, I am so proud of you! If you think you can do all your school work and your jobs around the house as well as visit the ladies at the nursing home, I can't see any reason to say no.

However, once a month, we will look at how you are coping with all of your commitments. You are not to let the ones slide that aren't as exciting as visiting the ladies at the nursing home."

Maggie felt as if all her Christmases had come at once and she said a heartfelt, "Thanks Mum, I promise!"

Laughing, Rose said, "Now is that all your news Maggie or is there more?"

Maggie had almost forgotten about the letter and happily said, "Oh yes, Grandma wrote the most amazing letter. How does she know what to say?"

"I don't know honey – she just does. May I read your letter?"

"Um, sure. I'll go and have my shower while you read it."

Maggie didn't want to be in the room when her mother read about how unhappy she had been with her life.

Rose stood in the middle of the kitchen, tears flowing freely, and sent out a silent prayer of thanks that

Maggie had turned a corner.

CHAPTER 4

15.9.2000 – Today's my 16th birthday. I wanted to do something different for my birthday, so I asked all the girls in my class to buy a jar or tube of their favourite hand cream and come to the nursing home at Dunedin Street at 2:00pm.

When I asked Mrs Parkinson if I could have my 16th birthday party at the nursing home she was quite surprised. But when I told her what I wanted to do and why, she smiled and said she'd ask Matron – who said, "Yes, of course!"

All the girls arrived at the nursing home at 2:00pm with their tubes or jars of hand cream. I suspect it was because they were curious rather than wanting to help me celebrate my birthday, but I didn't care. This was my first birthday party!!!

Mrs Parkinson had kindly arranged for everyone to meet outside the meeting room, and she kept the door shut until everyone arrived. When Maggie opened the door to the meeting room, it wasn't what they expected. Instead of party food, drinks and dance music, there were 16 white baskets on the table with a soft fluffy hand towel in each one. The hand towels were all different colours and looked spectacular.

All the girls looked at each other in confusion, then at the baskets and then at Maggie. She could see they were wondering – what kind of a party was this?

She laughed at the looks on their faces, then told them about her letter to her grandmother and how when she didn't get a reply instantly realised, with her mother's help, she was only thinking about herself. Seeing she had all the girls' attention, Maggie's confidence grew and she continued.

"I decided I wanted to do something in our community that took my attention off me for a time. This decision led me to the nursing home and Mrs Roberts.

I have loved coming to the nursing home so much I wanted to share the experience with all of you. I started my first day here with a basket just like this (picking up a basket with a pink fluffy hand towel in it) and a jar of rose scented hand cream.

Matron has very kindly agreed that all of you can

sit with one of the grandmothers who don't see their grandchildren. If you want to, while you chat to them, you can gently rub your hand cream into their hands and arms too, just like I did.

For my birthday, I wanted to give you all a gift. Not only the gift of the basket and soft fluffy hand towel, but the gift of giving your time and energy to someone who thought they would never be touched in this way again.

I sit quietly with my 'nursing home grandma' and ask her if she would like me to massage some luxurious hand cream into her hands and arms. Let me tell you they all say 'ooohhh, yes please dear'. Sometimes we talk, and other times we just feel what it feels like to massage and be massaged.

I have found it to be a very special time and thought

you might enjoy it, too."

There was a stunned silence for a full minute with everyone looking at each other not quite sure what to say. Maggie absently chewed the inside of her mouth looking around the room, waiting for someone to say something, anything. Eventually someone spoke awkwardly.

"Maggie, it sounds er, interesting. Um, thank you for inviting me." Shanna (the leader of the 'cool group') with a puzzled look, slowly turned around and included all the girls in the room with her arms, and changed 'me' to 'us'.

Shocked that Shanna even spoke, Maggie couldn't believe it. Even though she didn't seem sure about it, in that one sentence Shanna accepted the invitation to celebrate her birthday in this way on behalf of every girl in the class. Although Maggie wasn't part of the group, she didn't feel left out anymore and she didn't have to become a follower to do it.

The door to the meeting room had been left slightly open. Rose, Matron and Mrs Parkinson stood at the door looking through the crack to see what was happening.

They saw a confident young woman clearly destined to lead rather than be led.

"Okay, now for the fun part. There's a basket for everyone, take one from the table, put your hand cream on top of the hand towel and we'll go and meet our nursing home grandmas."

Shanna picked her basket first and turned to Maggie and said, "Have you really been coming here for six months?"

"Yeah, I have," said Maggie with a grin. "It has been inspirational. I've loved every minute of it. This is the reason I jump out of bed each morning and go to school because I know I'll be coming here in the afternoon."

"You know, I could tell there was something different about you. You've changed the way you dress, you've cut you hair – and Maggie, how much weight have you lost??? You're so skinny now! Now that I'm really looking at you, you've changed a lot – but, you know, I couldn't figure out what you've been doing until now. You're really happy, aren't you?"

Taken aback, Maggie turned to Shanna and said, "Yes I am, Shanna. Aren't you?"

Unexpectedly, Shanna's eyes filled with tears.

"No. I'm not. When I look at you and feel your enthusiasm and excitement for life and your happiness at giving to others, I can see how selfish and shallow I am and how thoughtless I've been. I haven't been very nice to you Maggie, and I'm really sorry about that. Does it sound selfish if I say I want to be happy like you?"

"Thank you for your apology. It really means a lot to me. Yes, I know how you're feeling. I felt like that when my mum helped me see how selfish and 'me, me, me' I was being. Shanna when you start giving to others and doing for others that awful feeling goes away. I think it's fantastic you want to be happy! Can we talk about this later?"

"Sure, thanks Maggie, I'd really like that. You

know, even though I have great friends, gorgeous clothes and go out when I want to, I'm still not happy! I can't figure it out. You don't have what I have and you look and sound so happy. Why is that? I want to know how to be happy like you!"

Shanna spoke with an intensity that surprised Maggie more than anything else that day.

[How amazing, Shanna wants to know something from me!!! I have to tell Grandma about this.]

Keeping the surprise from her face, Maggie said, "Ah, sure. If you like, we can talk later after the party or we can meet at my house one afternoon after I've been to the nursing home."

"Um, thanks," Shanna said awkwardly, more than a bit embarrassed by her outburst. She didn't know where that came from.

Maggie turned back to the group, saw everyone had their baskets and were waiting curiously to see what happened next. Confidently, Maggie said, "Okay, come on girls let's go and meet those lovely grandmothers who have been waiting all day for this treat!!!"

After an hour of blissful connection between elderly woman and young woman, all the girls said goodbye to their adopted "granny" amid whispers of promises to come again soon.

Mrs Parkinson ushered them all back into the meeting room. Maggie was the last to go in and she couldn't believe what she saw.

Tears filled her eyes and spilled over – she couldn't speak because her throat was full of emotion.

The room had been transformed into a real surprise birthday party with streamers, balloons, banners and music. Matron was standing in the corner. Her eyes sparkled with tears when she saw the wonder and delight on Maggie's face. This was her first real birthday party.

Rose was in another corner with Mrs Parkinson. They were both smiling from ear-to-ear pleased their plan was successful.

All the girls were shouting and cheering. It was great fun. There was delicious party food and hilarious party games.

All the girls were having a fabulous time. Maggie finally felt part of the 'cool group'. She realised too, Grandma was right, when she spoke to each of the girls individually they all said they felt different in some way. She wasn't alone in this feeling.

Ring, ring, ring!

Mrs Parkinson was ringing the reception bell. It sounded so out of place, but she certainly got everyone's attention.

"Girls, girls – Matron would like to say something to all of you and especially to you Maggie."

"Dear young women, what a delight it has been to have you all here today to celebrate Maggie's 16th birthday. When Maggie came here 6 months ago, although she was shy, a little awkward and nervous, we felt an angel had come to visit. And she continued to visit and blossom into this fine young woman before us now.

Today, we have had the pleasure of welcoming 16 young angels to the nursing home and we hope you will all come again and continue to come again, just like our angel Maggie here.

You have brought a breath of fresh air, sunshine and contagious energy into all our lives and you transformed the nursing home from a 'waiting station' into a 'vibrant home', full of life and energy. Thank you all very much! The change has been remarkable."

After speaking collectively to the girls, Matron turned her attention to Maggie, "HAPPY BIRTHDAY Maggie! What an inspiration you are to all of us. You've demonstrated true leadership today in bringing these young women together to experience something most wouldn't even think of, let alone do. Congratulations my dear from all of us at the nursing home. We hope you continue to share your time with our lovely ladies as the years roll by and you experience life's adventures with an open willing heart."

Everyone in the room looked at Maggie. She couldn't think or speak for a moment – she was so overwhelmed. With glistening eyes and shaking hands Maggie opened her arms to include everyone and said in a voice choked with emotion, "Thank you Matron and Mrs Parkinson and my new friends. This has been the best birthday ever. Thank you to my Grandma who inspired all of this and most of all thank you to my Mum.

Over the past six months, I've had a chance to truly appreciate everything you do for me. You are the best Mum ever and I love that you encourage me every day. If it hadn't been for your guidance and faith in me, I would never have recognised how selfish I was nor would I have had the courage to come here and experience this incredible journey. Thank you everyone for sharing this very special day with me.

Mum, I'm so grateful for your support, because I was very depressed 6 months ago. Making the decision to come to the nursing home turned my life around and now I'm the happiest I've ever been.

This is just the beginning. I hope everyone will keep coming to the nursing home and you'll tell your friends about it. Maybe they'd like to visit a grandmother in a nursing home near where they live and do what we're doing. Wouldn't that be incredible. We could start a movement!"

Everyone looked at Maggie waiting to see if she would say anything else, but she couldn't speak anymore. Suddenly everyone spontaneously started cheering and clapping loudly.

The party was a great success. When it ended, everyone went home a different girl from the one who arrived at 2:00pm.

CHAPTER 5

24.9.2000 – Shanna came over this afternoon.
I didn't think she really meant what she said at my
birthday party – that she wanted me to tell her how to
be happy. I didn't even know she knew where I lived!
It was a little weird to start with. It didn't take me long
to forget how horrible she can be. Today was another
extraordinary day.

There was a tentative knock at the front door.
Maggie wondered who it could be as they didn't usually
get visitors during the week. When she opened the door,

Shanna was standing there crying and looking very unhappy.

Surprised, Maggie immediately opened the door wider for her to come in and said, "Shanna, what's wrong?"

Shanna really started sobbing then and couldn't speak for a few minutes. When she had calmed down said, "My mother has kicked me out of home. She said she doesn't want anything more to do with me."

Really shocked and a little confused, Maggie said, "I'm sorry to hear that, but why have you come here? I didn't think you liked me or wanted anything to do with me."

Shanna started sobbing again because she knew Maggie was right – that is, until the birthday party. So much had happened since then. She didn't know where to start.

Maggie knew her mother would make a cup of hot Milo for Shanna and just listen. So that's what she did.

"Can I make you a hot Milo?"

"Uh uuuhhhh yes please," Shanna said nodding her head sadly.

Maggie made hot Milo for both of them and took Shanna into the garden to sit on the fairy bench It had a soothing effect on Shanna immediately.

Not feeling very confident of being able to help Shanna, but experiencing great compassion, Maggie invited her to tell her story and to start with whatever came into her mind.

"When I saw how kind your mother was and how much you respected and loved her, I knew I had missed out on a lot. I can't remember when I haven't fought with my mum. I don't remember ever feeling what I felt when I watched you and your mum together.

I went home from your party wanting to be nice to my mother, but she yelled at me as soon as I walked through the door and I forgot all about being nice to her. She found out I had been sneaking out at night and meeting up with my boyfriend in the park."

"Oh! What happened?"

"She told me I wasn't allowed to go anywhere except to school and she would drive me there and pick me up."

"Okay that doesn't seem so bad. What went

wrong?"

"Um, I still went out. I climbed out my window, across the roof and down the side of the house where I'd put the ladder."

"Shanna! You could have been killed!"

"That's what she said, too."

"And then what happened?"

"While I was at school she searched through my room and found some drugs and a box of condoms."

"Oh Shanna, I take it she was very angry with you."

"Angry isn't the word for it. She went ballistic and started throwing things at me. She said she'd had enough of my obnoxious and defiant behaviour and to get out of her house and not come back – EVER!"

Maggie was shocked. "Has this happened before?"

Shanna sheepishly nodded her head and said, "But this time it was different – I know she meant it. I was yelling and swearing back at her and told her I hated her and wished she wasn't my mother."

Maggie didn't know what to say – she felt way out of her depth, but knew her mum would know what to do.

"Shanna, I don't know what to say. I'm really shocked. I can't imagine what it would be like to experience what you've told me. All this time, I thought you had it all, and that's just not true. You helped me understand another lesson today. Everything is not what it seems.

Mum will be home from work soon. I think it would be best if we both talked to her about what's happened and see what she thinks."

Shanna looked anxiously at her and said, "Do you really think that's a good idea. Your mum knows how awful I've been to you since primary school. She might tell me to leave, too."

"I don't think so. She's a pretty cool mum. Nothing much seems to phase her."

They kept talking in the garden till Rose came home.

--

Rose arrived home to a quiet house. "That's strange," she thought, "Maggie should have been home from the nursing home by now. I hope nothing has happened to her!"

Rose stood at the back door calling out to see if she was in the garden. Maggie jumped up eagerly from the bench and called back, "Hi Mum. I'm in the fairy garden with Shanna", and started running along the path to the back door. Shanna slowly followed, afraid of facing Rose and telling her about her problem.

As Shanna walked around the orchid greenhouse, she saw Rose scoop Maggie into a loving hug. Her face full of smiles and her eyes full of questions. Rose looked up and saw Shanna awkwardly standing there. She beckoned her to come inside and share her day with her, just as she usually did with Maggie.

Shanna started to cry again. Rose looked at Maggie questioningly and then at Shanna with compassion. She opened her arms to Shanna who walked straight into them and received the hug like a drowning man given a lifeline.

"Oh dear," thought Rose, "something is terribly wrong here."

"Shanna love, what is it? What's happened?"

"I'm sorry Mrs Fraser, uuuhhhh, I've had a huge fight with my mother and she kicked me out of home. I know I haven't been very nice to Maggie, but when I saw you both at her birthday party, I knew you had something together that I've never had. I really need that right now. I'm so unhappy, I didn't know where else to go."

"But what about your father Shanna, surely he wouldn't let this happen?"

"My parents divorced when I was a baby and I haven't seen him since I was 7. Mum said he didn't want to see me anymore, but I'm starting to wonder whether that's true. I remember whenever she spoke to him on the phone or when I spent time with him, she always yelled at him. My mum yells a lot! And I suppose I learned to yell back just to be heard."

"Okay love, here's what we'll do. You can stay here with us tonight and I'll call your mother and let her know where you are."

Shanna's face brightened at this, but then it dropped at the thought of what her mother would say to Rose. Sensing her uneasiness, Rose put her arm around Shanna's shoulders, squeezed them and told her not to worry about anything.

"Maggie, can you take Shanna up to the spare room

and show her where the bathroom is etc. Give her a towel and you might like to find some pyjamas for her to wear. But before you go upstairs Shanna can you tell me your phone number at home please."

After the girls had gone upstairs, Rose telephoned Shanna's mother, Vivienne. It wasn't as pleasant as she hoped it would be. After telling Rose all the dreadful things Shanna had put her through, Vivienne said she wasn't welcome home and didn't care what became of her. She'd had enough!

In her most placating voice, Rose told Vivienne that Shanna would be staying at their place for now and gave her the telephone number in case she wanted to contact her.

When the girls came back downstairs Rose told Shanna she had spoken to her mother. She gently told her not to worry and that everything would turn out for the best.

"Don't worry love, you'll be taken care of. Your mother has packed a suitcase for you and I'll get Maggie's Dad to go around and collect it after dinner."

In the morning, the girls come downstairs to find Rose busy making pancakes for breakfast. There was a tablecloth on the table with cutlery and plates and four glasses of orange juice. As they arrived in the kitchen, Donald (Maggie's Dad) walked in from the back garden with the newspaper in his hand. He had been reading it in the sun while he waited for them to come down.

Shanna was stunned. She didn't think people really lived like this. They had never set the table in her house and when they ate it was on the lounge in front of the television. Also she had never seen her mother cook breakfast. She usually went to school without breakfast.

Rose put a plate of delicious pancakes in the middle of the table and told Shanna to start first. There were plenty for everyone and Shanna loved the maple syrup and ice cream first thing in the morning. Donald kept them all laughing with his adventurous stories from his youth.

When they had finished breakfast, Donald asked Shanna if she would mind if he had a word with Rose and Maggie alone. She had a sinking feeling in her stomach, but smiled brightly and went off to the bathroom to get ready for school.

Donald and Rose both turned to Maggie and spoke at the same time. They laughed and started again. Donald spoke this time.

"Maggie when I went to see Vivienne last night she was still very angry and I don't think she will be welcoming Shanna back into her house for some time. It is sad this is Shanna's reality at the moment. Your mum and I discussed it late into the night and with your approval, we would like to offer a home to Shanna for as long as she wants to say – that is, if she would like to stay.

Now before you say anything, it seems Shanna has been misbehaving with boys and drugs and we are concerned she may influence you. We are happy to offer our home to Shanna on the condition she honours our rules, does her share of the chores and participates with us as a family."

Maggie jumped around the kitchen trying not to scream. In a loud whisper, she shouted, "Are you really saying that Shanna can stay here with us! Like she would be my foster sister? And be part of our family?"

Donald grinned and looked at Rose who was also grinning. Clearly, the bullying didn't overshadow Maggie's feeling of wanting to be accepted by Shanna.

"Yes, that's exactly what we're saying. You better go and get Shanna and bring her down so we can invite her into the family."

Maggie ran to the bottom of the stairs and shouted, "Shanna come downstairs now!"

Hearing the excitement in Maggie's voice, Shanna didn't need any second bidding. She was already standing on the top step wondering what was being said downstairs.

Both girls walked into the kitchen together. Donald

asked everyone to sit down at the table again.

"Shanna after speaking with your mother last night, I realised you are in a very difficult situation. Rose and I discussed this at length last night and with Maggie's support, we would like to invite you to be part of our family for as long as you want to stay."

Shanna started to shake all over and burst into tears. She couldn't breathe and looked from one to the other to make sure they weren't playing a sick joke on her. She was stunned there were people in the world who would be so nice to someone as horrible as her. When she said this, Rose put her arms around her and gave her a big hug.

"Shanna honey – you're not horrible. You've had a troubled childhood and now you're being offered an opportunity to live in a home with an abundance of love. Sometimes out of the worst circumstances comes amazing gifts from God. We hope you will come and live with us and learn to love and be loved."

Donald spoke again. "Shanna your mother told me she found drugs and condoms in your room and you've been sneaking out at night. Although you have behaved this way at your mother's place, we don't accept that behaviour here.

Shanna don't be in too much of a hurry to grow up. You will have plenty of opportunity to grow in this home, but not through experimenting with drugs, sex and alcohol. You'll learn to grow through developing relationships, open communication, accepting responsibility for your actions, being held accountable, participating in group considerations about important decisions, respect of self and others and much more.

I know this is probably very overwhelming for you. Take as long as you need to decide. Shanna, would you like to join our family?"

She couldn't believe something this good would happen to her. She looked at Maggie whose face was brimming with happiness.

Through her tears and emotion, Shanna nodded her head vigorously and humbly said, "Ever since Maggie's birthday party I imagined one day I would feel loved like that, too. I never believed it would happen so soon though. Yes please, I would love to live with you all. I promise to behave myself. Especially if it means I can be this happy.

Thank you for accepting me into your home even though I've been horrible to Maggie which I am truly sorry for; I've been doing things you don't approve of and yet you still trust I'll do the right thing in the future. No one has ever done that for me before."

Maggie grabbed Shanna in a big hug and laughed and cried as she rocked back and forwards with her. Everyone was happy with the outcome.

CHAPTER 6

12.5.2001 – Today was Shanna's 17th birthday. Mum and I organised a surprise party for her. We had it in the back garden and Dad put coloured fairy lights through the garden. It was a fantastic party.

I'm so happy Shanna came to live with us. She's changed a lot and is really nice to everyone now. She seems happier, too. And it looks like her dream has come true!!!

Shanna decided she wanted to go to the movies with Maggie and a couple of their friends to celebrate her birthday. They saw a "girlie" movie and arrived home at 6:30pm expecting to have pizza for dinner and listen to music.

When they arrived home, the lights were out and the front door was locked. The girls looked at each other questioningly and shrugged a silent answer. After dropping the girls at the movies, Donald and Rose said they'd see them at home at 6:30pm with pizzas. Obviously, they hadn't arrived home yet.

Maggie found her key and opened the front door. Laughing, all the girls rushed inside, fighting over who was first in the bathroom.

As they made their way into the kitchen, the lights came on and 40 people jumped out of their hiding places shouting "Surprise!!! HAPPY BIRTHDAY SHANNA!!!" The kitchen had balloons floating on the ceiling, streamers everywhere, colourful decorations around the back door and fairy lights were strung throughout the garden. It looked like a magical world.

Shanna looked around the room at all the happy, smiling faces and finally came to Rose and Donald who were standing together looking and feeling very proud. Shanna ran over to them and gave them both a huge hug. She was overwhelmed, but thrilled at the same time.

Six months ago Shanna would never have imagined celebrating her 17th birthday like this. She squeezed Donald and Rose again and from her heart quietly said, "Thank you so much for accepting me into your home and making me feel loved and welcome. I love you both so much. I don't know what would have happened to me without you and Maggie."

These words were the best gift she could have given them. This was the first time Shanna had openly expressed her feelings for Donald and Rose and to hear her say she loved them was a special moment. Donald gave her a quick squeeze back and said, "Shanna you are a gift to us. We always wanted more children, but it wasn't to be. You are the extra family we couldn't have ourselves. We love you dearly and we know Maggie does, too."

The party seemed to be taking off around them with everyone laughing and music playing loudly. Rose caught Maggie's eye and she nodded slightly. Shanna saw this and wondered what was happening. Maggie crossed the room and joined them.

Donald ushered Shanna, Maggie and Rose out the back door, closed it quietly and led them through the light filled garden down to the fairy garden. There was a man sitting on the bench watching them come towards him. He slowly stood up as they came closer.

Shanna looked at him and then questioningly

at Donald – tears filled her eyes and her right hand clutched at her heart. Donald nodded his head and gestured for her to go to him.

Shanna stepped forward falteringly, "Daddy, is it really you?"

With tears rolling down his face, but smiling broadly he nodded and opened his arms to her. "Yes, baby girl it's me." Shanna ran the last few metres into his open arms and sobbed her heart out. Her father, Richard, wasn't far from doing the same and he held her tightly as if he would never let her go again.

Donald, Rose and Maggie all looked at each other, grinned and walked back along the fairy light path to the kitchen. No one had even noticed they'd been missing.

When she could talk, Shanna asked the question she'd been wanting to ask for 10 years, "Daddy, why did you leave me?"

"I have asked myself this question often over the years and my only answer is I thought it would make life easier for you. I thought you would be happier if you didn't have to see your mother and I fighting all the time and experience the drama she created when I wanted to see you.

I am really sorry I didn't fight for you, but I didn't know what else to do. Your mother convinced me you were better off without me in your life. She said I was confusing you.

We owe a really big thank you to Donald, Rose and Maggie. Maggie told her parents she thought it would be a great birthday present to find me and see if I

wanted to be part of your life again. My God, Shanna –
I thought I would never see you again."

Richard had dreamt of this moment for 10 years
and couldn't quite believe it was happening. He never
meant to hurt Shanna by leaving and he wasn't sure if
she wanted him back in her life. He hesitantly asked
her, "Angel, do you think I could be your Dad again? It
will be different now I promise!"

Shanna pulled out of his arms, looked deep into his
eyes (he felt as though she had touched his soul) and
said, "Daddy, I couldn't let you go again even if you
wanted me to. I have asked for this day since the last
day I saw you. I am amazed Maggie could feel what
was in my heart because I haven't told anybody my
secret dream."

They hugged again. Then happily grabbing hold of

her father's hand, Shanna led the way back to the party going on in the kitchen.

Donald, Rose and Maggie were thrilled to see Richard and Shanna holding hands and looking so happy. This was their cue to move the party into the other half of the garden. Maggie led the way like the Pied Piper along the fairy lit path to the grass clearing. Everyone erupted into cheers. There was a muslin tent with tables filled with delicious food and bins filled with crushed ice and different drinks.

One of the boys from school (whose dream was to be a DJ) had set up his equipment and he played a mixture of music everyone loved. A temporary dance floor had been set up on the grass next to the tent and it was a magical night for everyone.

Shanna felt as if she was the luckiest girl in the

world.

Richard couldn't think where to begin or how to thank Donald and Rose for taking care of Shanna when Vivienne had kicked her out of home. They all agreed words weren't necessary. Each understood the love a parent experiences for their child and they all felt that for Shanna.

During the 10 years Richard had been gone from Shanna's life he had become successful in business and remarried. All this time, he had been living in the same city as Shanna and she didn't know.

Shanna was thrilled to have her father back in her life, even though she was afraid he would leave her again. She spoke about this to Rose who assured her time would heal that fear and to live in the now, trust what she was feeling and enjoy it.

The day after her birthday, Richard took Shanna out for the day. They went to the beach and walked for kilometres along the sand, letting the water swirl around their feet as they talked and talked, catching up on all their lost years.

Richard knew he was putting off what he wanted to tell Shanna because he wasn't sure how she would react. Finally, he took a deep breath, asked Shanna to sit on the sand with him and turned to her with eyes filled with conflicting emotions. Hope, fear, sadness and hope again.

Shanna wondered what was going on and began to feel scared.

Richard said, "Angel, I have something to tell you. I met a beautiful, kind, gentle woman. She is everything I wanted in a woman and she finally agreed to marry me

5 years ago. We now have two beautiful children, Kara who is 3 and Dylan who is 6 months old.”

Before he could say anything more, Shanna had thrown her arms around his neck shouting, “Get out!!!! You mean I have a baby sister and brother, too? I can’t believe you are telling me this. I couldn’t have asked for a better birthday. To be with my father again and to have more family to love. When can I see them??? Oh, um, what is your wife’s name? Do you think she would like me? Does she want to meet me? Does she know about me?”

Richard laughed and hugged her back.

“What a relief! I was worried you wouldn’t be happy about me remarrying and having more children. Maybe that was another reason why I didn’t try to find you again.

And yes, Kate does know about you and she is dying to meet you. Kara knows she has a big sister, but she doesn't really understand what that means yet."

Jumping up from the sand, she held her hand out to Richard and pulled him up, too. Barely able to contain her excitement, she shouted to the world, "I … can't … believe … it!!!" Then she turned to Richard with tears streaming down her face and said, "Oh Dad, I'm so happy!!! Can we go and meet them now?"

Shanna loved her new family and they loved her back just as much.

As Shanna was in her final year of high school, it was agreed she would live with Donald, Rose and Maggie during the week and spend the weekends with Richard, Kate, Kara and Dylan.

Maggie was thrilled with this arrangement, as she didn't lose the sister she had always longed for and Shanna felt she had the best of everything – 2 sets of loving parents, 2 sisters and a brother.

Maggie, Donald and Rose became part of Richard's family, too.

CHAPTER 7

28.6.2001 – I'm starting to understand that life doesn't stay wonderful every day – and that's just how it is.

When I went to visit Mrs Roberts today she didn't know me. Mum told me this might happen, but I really wasn't expecting it. I was shocked at how hurt and sad I felt that she didn't remember me. My first thought was how could you forget something so special. But she did.

Today was hard.

Maggie knocked gently on Mrs Roberts' door as usual before opening it and walked confidently over to the bed. She didn't notice anything was different today as she was intent on putting a beautiful bunch of flowers from their garden on the desk beside Mrs Roberts' bed.

She heard a soft, "Ahhhemmm. Cccccaaannn I hhheelllpp you?"

Maggie turned around with her usual beaming smile ready to say a bright hello when she noticed Mrs Roberts looked afraid of her. She reached out her hand to touch her arm in concern but stopped when she saw Mrs Roberts instinctively shrink away.

Maggie felt wounded that Mrs Roberts would treat her this way after all they had shared together. She wondered what she had done wrong. This was so unlike her, she usually looked forward to Maggie's visits.

Suddenly, Mrs Roberts started shouting (as best she could) at her, "Get away from me! You thief! You've stolen my jewels! I'll get the police! Don't you go anywhere!" and pressed the buzzer with every word she spoke.

Maggie stood there looking dumbfounded. Her mouth dropped open and she forgot to close it again. "What on earth had gotten into Mrs Roberts," she thought.

Mrs Parkinson heard the commotion and came rushing into the room to see a distressed Maggie and an agitated Mrs Roberts.

Mrs Parkinson soothed, "There, there Mrs Roberts, it's okay – this is Maggie. She comes to sit with you every week and rubs your hands and arms with beautiful hand cream. Do you remember?"

"NNNNooooo. No, get her away!"

Mrs Parkinson gently shook her head at Maggie and asked her to meet her at reception.

"It's alright, she's leaving. You're safe now."

But Mrs Roberts was still agitated and a nurse came and gave her an injection She went to sleep, looking frail, yet peaceful.

--

Maggie was very distressed when Mrs Parkinson caught up with her at reception.

"What just happened in there? Did I do something

wrong? Does she hate me?”

"Maggie dear, you haven’t done anything wrong and no she doesn’t hate you. She simply doesn’t remember you. She is deteriorating in her mind, love. She seems to drift between worlds or memories. We really aren’t sure what actually happens in those episodes.

"Should I stop coming to visit her?”

"No, no love. Some days she will know you and will love that you are still visiting. But be prepared that sometimes she won’t remember you and it’s nothing you’ve done. Okay?”

Maggie felt sad and mutely nodded her head as her throat was tight with emotion.

"Look love, unfortunately, this is part of the aging process. No one wants it to happen to them, but when the heart is strong it keeps beating and the rest of the body starts breaking down around it. This is what's happening with Mrs Roberts. She doesn't know she's forgetting and that my dear is the gift of ignorance.

You've brought much joy and love into her life this past couple of years and I'm sure they've been some of the best years she's had.

Maggie, please keep coming to visit like you've always done. Trust me, you'll share more happy moments with her. We don't know for sure how long she'll continue in this way, but your love brightens up her day when she remembers who you are."

She left the nursing home sadder than she'd been since she started going when she was 15.

--

Maggie didn't want Mrs Robert to forget her! She went home and made a collage of photos from when she was a baby, right through to the present. She put it in a beautiful frame. The following week when it was her day to see Mrs Roberts she took the gift with her. Maggie's heart melted as Mrs Roberts' face lit up when she walked through the door.

Today was a good day.

She sat beside Mrs Roberts and handed her the gift which was wrapped in light pink tissue paper and a beautiful deep pink ribbon.

Mrs Roberts' eyes went wide with surprise and delight. "What is this for Maggie? It's not my birthday is it?

Maggie laughed. "No, it's not your birthday. I wanted to give you something so you could remember me when I'm not here. I wanted to tell you I love you and appreciate all your stories about when you were young and the adventures you've had throughout your life.

I hope my life is as full as yours and I get to experience as many things as you."

Deeply touched, Mrs Roberts said through a watery smile, "Why Maggie dear that has to be one of the nicest things anyone has ever said to me. Thank you. Now, what have we here?"

As excited as a little girl, Mrs Roberts tore the ribbon off and ripped the wrapping paper in her rush to see her gift. "Oh my dear – how beautiful! Now I can see all of you. What a lovely child you are! Thank you dear. Every day I will treasure this."

She put the photo frame on the bedside table where she could see it even when she was lying down.

Maggie was moved by Mrs Roberts' response to her gift. She didn't expect to feel that way.

--

Maggie went home knowing she only had a little bit longer to love Mrs Roberts and she was okay with that. She finally understood what her mother had been saying about living each moment and experiencing joy and happiness even though you know there is sadness to come.

CHAPTER 8

26.10.2001 – School finished today. It's scary and exciting at the same time. The security of school and childhood is gone forever. Now, I have to wait to see whether I get into university or not!!!

Who would ever have believed 2 years ago that Shanna and I would not only become good friends, but we would be living together and I became part of the 'cool group'. It has been an incredible year.

27.10.2001 – I tried to stay in bed late today. All my exams were done and that's how I wanted to celebrate the closing of one door and the opening of another. But it wasn't to be.

Today my world changed forever.

Maggie woke briefly feeling the sunlight on her face and then drifted back into deep sleep and happy dreams until being dragged back to reality by the incessant – ring ring … ring ring … ring ring … ring ring of the telephone.

"Grrr, looks like Mum isn't going to answer that!" Maggie grumbled to herself.

Padding down the hall to the phone, still half asleep, Maggie answered it with a sleepy, "Hello."

"Is that you dear, it's Mrs Parkinson from the nursing home."

Maggie suddenly became fully awake and concerned, "Yes, Mrs Parkinson its Maggie. What's wrong? You've never rung me at home before."

"Maggie dear, can you come? Its Mrs Roberts. She's slipping away and we thought you would want to come and say goodbye."

Tears welled in Maggie's eyes, spilled over and rolled down her face. She managed to splutter, "Oh Mrs Parkinson. Of course, I want to come. I'll be there as soon as I can. She won't die before I get there will she?"

Maggie held her breath waiting for the answer.

"No dear. You have a little bit of time."

She quickly had a shower, threw on some clothes

and brushed her hair back off her face into a ponytail. She ran downstairs looking for her mother and as she reached the kitchen Rose came through the back door with an armful of fresh flowers from the garden. She took one look at Maggie's face and knew something had deeply upset her. Putting the flowers on the bench she opened her arms and Maggie ran into them sobbing.

"Hey, Maggie love what is it? Are you ill? What's happened?"

"Uuuuuhhhh, Mrs Parkinson just called to say that Mrs Roberts is slipping away, uuuhhh and would … I … like to come down to say goodbye."

"Oh dear I was expecting this would happen sooner rather than later. How do you feel about going down to be with Mrs Roberts?"

"Mum, I want … to … go. But I'm … afraid. What's it like … when someone … dies? Is it … scary?"

"Darling death and dying isn't anything to be afraid of. I suspect Mrs Roberts will be breathing less often than normal and will appear to be drifting in and out of sleep. Eventually, her breathing will appear to stop and start and may even have a rattle to it, and then she will slip away as her last breath is breathed. I expect it will be a peaceful passing.

You have brought great joy to Mrs Roberts over the past couple of years and I'm sure she would like to see you if she is still conscious. If she isn't, she will most definitely feel your presence.

If you feel you can go and sit with her awhile, I'm sure you will be really glad you did."

"Uuuuhhh, thanks Mum. I don't feel so scared now."

"Come on. I know it's just a short way, but I'll drive you down there. Why don't we take these flowers from the garden and put them in her room? She might smell them as we bring them in."

"That would be nice Mum and I would really like it if you could come and sit with me."

"Of course darling, come on then let's go."

Maggie was grateful her mother came to the nursing home with her. They were there in no time at all. Mrs Parkinson met them at the entrance. A sweet smile appeared on her face when she saw them coming through the glass sliding doors.

Maggie escaped into her mind, "I wonder if it is because I know someone is going to die in the nursing home today that it feels different somehow. Is it just me who feels this or does everyone feel something is happening today? It isn't a sad feeling, just a different feeling."

"Hello Maggie dear and you too, Rose. Thanks for coming so quickly. It'll be soon."

Maggie turned stricken eyes towards her mother.

"Come on darling, it'll be alright. I'll sit with you."

They walked quietly into Mrs Roberts' lovely pink room. She opened her eyes slightly as they entered the room and her face lit up when she saw Maggie coming towards her. Maggie's heart melted and she stopped for a moment expecting Mrs Roberts to speak. But she didn't. Her eyelids slowly closed and the light slipped out of her face. Maggie looked at her mother to see if it had happened and Rose gently shook her head.

Mrs Parkinson got a vase for the flowers and put them where Mrs Roberts could see them, if she opened her eyes again.

Maggie couldn't think – she wanted her mother to tell her what to do.

Whispering softly, Rose said, "Darling, tell Mrs Roberts anything you want to say to her. Even if she doesn't open her eyes, she can still hear you."

Maggie reached for Mrs Roberts' hand and lightly stroked it, like when she used to massage it with hand cream. She softly said, "Granny Roberts." And her eyelids fluttered, but didn't open. "You have been a real gift to me. Thank you so much for letting me spend my afternoons with you and for all your stories which I loved. I will always remember you. You will always be in my heart. I love you so much."

Rose touched Maggie's arm and whispered, "Tell Mrs Roberts when she slips between this world and the next to go straight Home. She's not to look to the left or the right, she's to shoot like an arrow straight up and Home to Source. That's where she's always wanted to be and now is the time to go straight there. Tell her to follow the light all the way Home."

Rose told Maggie to touch the top of Mrs Roberts' head, tap it lightly and say, "Go Home, shoot straight up to the Light. There is no more to do here."

Maggie whispered again very softly in her ear, "It's time to go Home Granny Roberts. Go Home now.

Home to Source."

Rose and Maggie sat quietly for a time and Mrs Roberts' breathing became shallow. She seemed to stop breathing altogether for a bit and then she would take a big shaky breath before it became shallow again. It sounded like her airways were filling with fluid. They crackled and bubbled as her chest rose and fell intermittently with each faulty breath.

Suddenly the room was silent and filled with a peaceful feeling. Maggie looked at Mrs Roberts' chest. It wasn't moving anymore. She looked at her mother, silently questioning. Rose gently nodded her confirmation. Maggie looked back at Mrs Roberts' face and before her eyes all the wrinkles left her face. She seemed to glow from the inside out. Oh, how beautiful she looked.

Stillness settled over the room. Rose quietly slipped out the door to let Matron know that Mrs Roberts had died. She was gone a little while, but Maggie didn't notice.

She looked so peaceful and beautiful. Maggie instinctively reached out to the lovely bunch of flowers Rose had collected from the garden that morning and broke a pink cosmos off at the top of the stem. She leaned over and gently placed it on Mrs Roberts' heart with a prayer, "Dear Granny Roberts, I place this flower on your heart centre in honour of you and the joy you have brought into my life and the lives of all those who came before me. I know you have returned Home now. You will always be in my heart. I love you."

Maggie tenderly touched her fingers to Mrs Roberts' now young face in a gesture of love and farewell.

Rose returned to the room at that moment and smiled as she saw the pink cosmos on Mrs Roberts' heart. Without speaking, she reached into the bunch of flowers and picked a white flower, placed it on Mrs Roberts' throat and said, "Dear Granny Roberts, I place this flower at your throat centre in honour of you and all the wisdom you have shared with Maggie over the past two years. Thank you from the bottom of my heart for all the love and kindness you have given to her and others throughout your life."

Watching, Maggie's eyes welled with tears that spilled over and ran down her face unchecked. She heard a noise behind her and turned around to see Shanna and the rest of the girls from her class standing in the doorway.

While she was out Rose telephoned Shanna at her father's place who then called another girl who called another until they were all told that Mrs Roberts had died. Amazingly, they all came straight away to say goodbye.

They saw that Rose and Maggie had placed a flower on Granny Roberts' heart and throat. With an unspoken question and an unspoken reply, first Shanna and then all of the other girls came into the room one at a time, picked a flower from the bunch in the vase beside the bed and placed it on Granny Roberts' body somewhere with a prayer.

After everyone had placed a flower on her body, Rose softly chanted an exquisite devotional song she had written. The room felt peaceful and appeared to brighten for a time until they could no longer feel her presence.

She looked magnificent in her death covered in

flowers which had been given with great love. The girls left the room and Rose, Maggie and Shanna sat for a little bit longer just feeling before they quietly left, too.

All the girls from Maggie's class were sitting in the meeting room where they had celebrated her surprise 16th birthday party over a year ago. Some of the girls were crying and others looked like they were numb with shock.

Rose glanced around the room at them all and then explained to the girls what she had said to Maggie before they went into Granny Roberts' room earlier in the day.

"Today you have participated in the passing of a wonderful woman – Granny Roberts. Your sensitivity to the moment has been remarkable. Through your love and prayers sending her on her way you have helped

her transition through the death process and on her way
Home.

I don't know what prompted Maggie to place the
flower on Granny's heart, nor do I understand what
happened after that with everyone placing a flower on
her body and offering a prayer. I do know she looks
beautiful, feels beautiful and through all of your efforts
you have transformed the death of Granny Roberts
from a sad moment into an incredibly beautiful, sacred
moment. I can feel all of your connections to her and to
God right now.

Naturally there will be a grieving process. You have
all demonstrated a maturity and compassion I have
not witnessed before in such a circumstance. You are
amazing young women who today began the transition
from 'protected school environment' into the real world.

Participating in Granny's transition has been a wonderful gift which you can share with the world. Death is acceptable and it is a sacred occasion for the one transitioning and for those who continue to live another day.

Thank you for making Granny Roberts' passing such a momentous and sacred one.

I feel sure what you witnessed today will provide a healing anchor in your hearts for the times when this occurs again in your lives. I trust you will have the wisdom, in the midst of your grief on those occasions, to lead your family and friends in the sacred ceremony you participated in today."

By now everyone was crying, but not with sadness. In everyone's eyes there was a sparkle of awe for the mystery of what's been and what will be.

CHAPTER 9

*31.10.2001 – It is now four days since Granny
Roberts died. I have never been to a funeral before and
I'm not sure if I want to go. What will happen? How
will I feel? Will anyone else be there?*

The sky was full of clouds. It seemed a very sad
day indeed with even the weather mourning the loss of
Granny Roberts.

It was Maggie's first funeral and she didn't know
what to expect. Understandably, she was afraid.

She looked at all the people. Where did they all come from?

All the girls from her class were there with their mums and some of the dads, too. There were some of the nurses from the nursing home and, of course, Matron and Mrs Parkinson. And some of the ladies from the nursing home. The ones who could still walk.

It was wonderful that so many people had come to say goodbye. Maggie had thought there would only be a small group of people at Granny Roberts' funeral and this was more upsetting for her than anything else. Instead, it looked like the chapel would be crowded.

Everyone lined up patiently to sign the white leather guest book before going into the chapel. Granny's favourite song was playing – Amazing Grace. Maggie cried with happiness thinking everything was so beautiful and perfect.

Mrs Parkinson said Maggie and her parents and Shanna and her family could sit in the front row, as Granny Roberts didn't have any family left alive to sit there. Everyone was really touched by this gesture.

At the front of the chapel was a shiny white coffin with a magnificent wreath of pink roses and camellia greenery laid out on top. Even then, it didn't seem real.

Maggie drifted off into her own world, "This is it. It really is the final goodbye!"

The Minister was talking, but Maggie was somewhere else remembering the lovely times they had together. With a start, she heard her name being called.

"And now we have Maggie who is going to read a

special poem for Granny Roberts. Would you like to come up now Maggie?"

With shaking legs and lungs that seemed to forget to work Maggie walked up to the front of the chapel. She managed that okay, but turning to look at everyone in the congregation she froze, overwhelmed by the moment. Her eyes welled up and she couldn't speak. She tried again, but the words couldn't get past the lump in her throat. Everyone was looking at her – willing her to get through her fear and sorrow. She closed her eyes and said a heartfelt silent prayer to Granny Roberts, "Granny, I need your help. Please, please help me read this poem to you now."

Maggie opened her eyes and took a deep breath all the way in and all the way out. She tried to speak again and this time her voice worked.

"I've got an angel in my corner

My Granny put it there

I come to it in gladness or when I'm in despair.

It's been there nearly all my life

Since I was quite small

It often shows me mountains are only mole hills

after all.

My granny said, "If you ever need me, I'll always

be around.

Though you will never see me and I'll never make a

sound.

But you'll feel a sense of comfort whenever you

think of me.

I'll be your guardian angel wherever you may be."

If these words were ever spoken, I really do not

know.

But in my imagination, I believed it to be so.

I put these thoughts out of my mind.

The years just rolled away.

Then one night when I was troubled, I began to
pray.

That night in dreams she came to me.

She stood beside my bed,

"Don't forget the angel in the corner"

are the very words she said.

I'm older now and wiser,

and life has produced some tangles.

But over and above all else,

I do believe in Angels."

Maggie stood there letting the words of the poem
sink in before continuing.

"Granny Roberts shared this poem with me often
over the past two years. She wrote it when she was
a young woman and it brought her great comfort
throughout her life. I know she would have loved for it
to be read today."

Now that the reading was over Maggie felt shaky inside again and had an urgent need to sit down before she fell down and embarrassed herself. She quickly made her way back to her seat, her heart thumping in her chest. As she reached her pew, she stumbled on the carpet and almost fell into the seat next to her mother.

Someone else got up to speak, but Maggie didn't know who they were and tuned out.

Still thinking about Granny Roberts, Maggie looked up at the ceiling and saw a stained glass window in the slope of the roof. She thought, what a shame it's a cloudy day today. Suddenly, the clouds parted and the sun shone straight through the gap in the clouds, through the glass window and around Maggie – no one else!

Maggie disappeared into her own world again.

"What an incredible thing to happen. I bet that's Granny Roberts come to say a last goodbye."

She touched her mother's hand gently and pointed to the ray of sunlight.

Rose looked up, smiled and slightly nodded her head to Maggie's unspoken question. She didn't say anything though.

Rose kindly brought Maggie's attention back to the service. The Minister was saying his final words, the curtains drew back and the coffin slowly moved behind the curtains before they closed again.

Maggie looked at the curtains blankly and then at her mother. Her mind screamed out, "That's it! All I have now are my memories!" A single tear rolled down Maggie's cheek as she sat there, just staring at the closed curtains.

Rose let her be, knowing in her heart she would be alright in time.

31.10.2001 (cont) – I'm so glad I went to the funeral today. It was a beautiful service – especially when the Minister invited everyone to come up to the coffin to say a last goodbye. There was a bowl of deep pink rose petals on a table at each end of the coffin and anyone who wanted to, slowly walked to the coffin in two rows and sprinkled a handful of rose petals on it before sitting down again.

It was perfect.

She would have loved it.

I can still remember what the rose petals felt like

before I sprinkled them over the coffin and said my last goodbye.

I'll never forget Granny Roberts, the 'cool group' or the rest of the girls in my class.

Granny Roberts' death was a milestone in all our lives and through her I now have a new sister and another family to love.

Julie Lewin is a medical intuitive, leader of women, mentor and author residing in Australia with her husband. She has appeared on the television show "The Extraordinary" performing remarkable medical intuitive readings. Julie is a renowned healer, Founder of AreekeerA® healing modality and teacher who inspires others with her desire for life and her ability to beat the odds. A lover of sunshine, nature and the beauty of life, she is a source of inspiration to many.

www.julielewin.com

www.ingramcontent.com/pod-product-compliance
Lightning Source LLC
Chambersburg PA
CBHW071527100726
47908CB00004B/1318